Machines at Work

Snowplows

by Cari Meister

Bullfrog Books

Ideas for Parents and Teachers

Bullfrog Books let children practice reading informational text at the earliest reading levels. Repetition, familiar words, and photo labels support early readers.

Before Reading
- Discuss the cover photo. What does it tell them?
- Look at the picture glossary together. Read and discuss the words.

Read the Book
- "Walk" through the book and look at the photos. Let the child ask questions. Point out the photo labels.
- Read the book to the child, or have him or her read independently.

After Reading
- Prompt the child to think more. Ask: Have you ever seen a snowplow? Was it at work?

Bullfrog Books are published by Jump!
5357 Penn Avenue South
Minneapolis, MN 55419
www.jumplibrary.com

Library of Congress Cataloging-in-Publication Data

Names: Meister, Cari, author.
Title: Snowplows / by Cari Meister.
Other titles: Bullfrog books. Machines at work.
Description: Minneapolis, MN : Jump!, Inc., 2017.
Series: Machines at work | "Bullfrog Books."
Audience: Ages 5–8. | Audience: K to grade 3.
Includes bibliographical references and index.
Identifiers: LCCN 2016002946 (print)
LCCN 2016011621 (ebook)
ISBN 9781620313695 (hardcover: alk. paper)
ISBN 9781620314876 (paperback)
ISBN 9781624964169 (ebook)
Subjects: LCSH: Snowplows—Juvenile literature.
Snow removal—Juvenile literature.
Classification: LCC TD868 .M45 2016 (print)
LCC TD868 (ebook) | DDC 629.225—dc23
LC record available at http://lccn.loc.gov/2016002946

Editor: Jenny Fretland VanVoorst
Series Designer: Ellen Huber
Book Designer: Leah Sanders
Photo Researchers: Kirsten Chang, Leah Sanders

Photo Credits: All photos by Shutterstock except: age fotostock, 22; Davide Calabresi/Shutterstock.com; Getty, 14–15, 20–21; iStock, cover, 8–9, 10–11, 12, 13; Rezaks/Dreamstime.com; Thinkstock, 16–17.

Printed in the United States of America at Corporate Graphics in North Mankato, Minnesota.

Table of Contents

Snowplows at Work

Wow!
Look at all the snow.

The road is a mess.
Cars slip. Cars slide.
It is not safe.

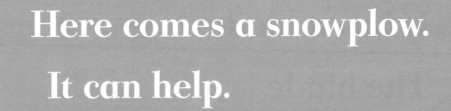

Here comes a snowplow.

It can help.

It has a blade.
The blade
scrapes the snow.

blade

bed

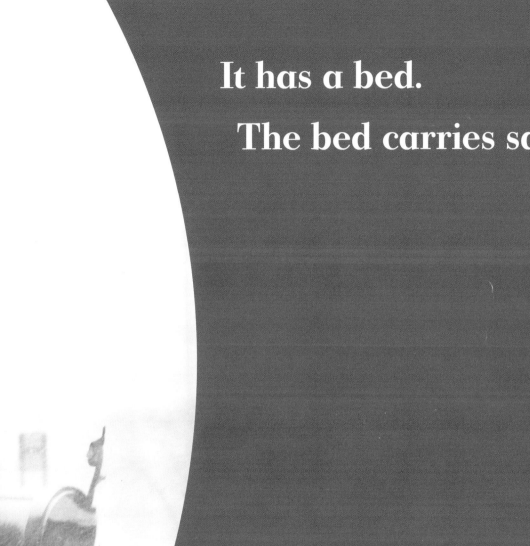

It has a bed.

The bed carries sand.

It has a spinner.

spinner

12

The spinner puts sand on the road.

Now it is not slippery.

Snowplows have lights that flash.

That way people see them.

Oh, no!

The runway
is full of snow.

The airplane
cannot take off.

Here comes a snowplow.

It pushes the snow.

It puts down salt.

Now the airplane can go.

Snowplows do good work!

Parts of a Snowplow

bed
The area of a truck that holds things, like salt and sand.

spinner
The part at the back of the bed that spins to release salt or sand from the bed and onto the road.

cab
The part of the truck where the driver sits; the driver can control the blade from the cab.

blade
The heavy piece of metal that is attached to the front; it is used to push snow.

Picture Glossary

runway
The long road that an airplane uses to pick up speed.

scrape
To remove something using a tool.

salt
Salt is put on roads to help melt ice and snow.

take off
To leave the ground and fly.

Index

To Learn More

Learning more is as easy as 1, 2, 3.

1) Go to www.factsurfer.com

2) Enter "snowplows" into the search box.

3) Click the "Surf" button to see a list of websites.

With factsurfer.com, finding more information is just a click away.